anythink

D0457799

The
MYSTERIOUS MAKERS
of Shaker Street

# THE HOLE NINE YARDS

The Mysterious Makers of Shaker Street
is published by Stone Arch Books,
A Capstone Imprint
1710 Roe Crest Drive
North Mankato, Minnesota 56003
www.mycapstone.com



Cataloging-in-Publication Data is available on the Library of Congress website.

ISBN: 978-1-4965-4679-1 (library binding)
ISBN: 978-1-4965-4683-8 (paperback)
ISBN: 978-1-4965-4687-6 (eBook PDF)

Summary: Shaker Street residents wake up to find holes all over their yards, and the Mysterious Makers decide to investigate.

Design Elements: Shutterstock: Master3D, PremiumVector

Designer: Tracy McCabe

Printed in Canada.
010382F17

The
MYSTERIOUS MAKERS
of Shaker Street

# THE HOLE NINE YARDS

by Stacia Deutsch
illustrated by Robin Boyden

STONE ARCH BOOKS
a capstone imprint

Shaker Street
TINA MARIE'S HOUSE
MRS. PATTERSON'S HOUSE
FOR SALE
SHAKER STREET BANK

MICHAEL'S HOUSE
MAKER SHACK
RS. THORNE'S HOUSE
HASSAN'S HOUSE
IV'S HOUSE
LEO'S HOUSE

# CHAPTER ONE

Michael Wilson couldn't sleep. He lay in bed, staring at the ceiling. "Why won't it work?" he muttered out loud to himself.

"Michael, go to sleep already," his best friend Leo Hammer said from the top bunk bed in Michael's room. Leo's dad was out of town for work, so Leo was staying with Michael for the weekend. "Your busy brain is keeping me awake."

"I know! It's terrible. My brain's keeping *me* awake too," Michael said. He rubbed his head. "I just don't understand why the telescope won't work. I'm positive that I made it right."

Michael looked across the room to where a long cardboard tube sat on his computer desk. Next to the tube were two lenses from two magnifying glasses that Michael's science teacher had given him.

He also had scissors and tape. Those were the things he knew he needed. But when he put it all together, the telescope didn't work. Everything appeared fuzzy and out of focus. *Why?*

Michael ran a hand over his short brown hair and muttered, "There has to be a way . . ."

"Dude, some people need their beauty sleep," Leo complained. He yawned and sat up in bed. His long, sand-colored hair was standing up in a thousand directions. "If you want me to look up telescopes on the Internet, then maybe we can —"

"No," Michael cut him off. "No, thanks."

Michael and Leo, along with Michael's cousin Liv, liked to make things. Liv and Michael's moms were sisters, and they were both ten years old. Leo was nine. Since all three of them lived on Shaker Street, they called themselves the Makers of Shaker Street.

When they were making things, if there was a problem, they always worked together to figure out the solution. They were a great team, but this time, Michael was determined to find an answer on his own.

"I'll figure it out," he said surely.

"Figure it out faster," Leo said, crashing back against his pillow. "This is supposed to be a fun sleepover. Key word is *sleep*."

"Sorry," Michael said, climbing out of bed. "I'm just going to try rearranging things one more time. Maybe if I put the pieces together in a different order . . ." He scooped up the parts and started to tape one of the lenses to the end of the tube. "I could turn the tube around. Would the other side work better? Maybe I —"

"Dude!" Leo complained. "You're talking to yourself." He tossed his pillow at Michael's head. It missed.

"Oh, sorry," Michael said. He did that when he was thinking really hard. "I'll go downstairs." He handed Leo back the pillow.

"Yippee," Leo said. "I was just getting into the best dream. We were in a strange village where there was this awesome house made of cookies. It had candy decorations."

"Like the witch's house in *Hansel and Gretel*?" Michael said, gathering his supplies. "I'd suggest you don't eat the house."

"Well, now you've ruined everything," Leo moaned. "It was the best dream ever. You turned it into a nightmare!"

"It's your dream," Michael said as he opened his bedroom door. "Change the ending."

"Yeah," Leo said in a soft voice. "I'm going to dream that I get to eat that whole house and be gone before the witch comes back." He gave a happy snore and fell back to sleep.

Michael chuckled to himself, then slipped into the darkened hallway. His parents were asleep, so he tiptoed past their bedroom to the stairs. He was heading down when an old man's voice stopped him in his tracks.

"Where ya headed, whippersnapper?" Grandpa Henry whispered.

Michael jumped. He was surprised that Grandpa was awake this late.

"I'm working on a project, Grandpa," Michael explained. He showed him the pieces of the telescope.

*"Hmmm."* Grandpa Henry was eighty years old with wild gray hair and a lot of wrinkles. He was Michael's dad's dad, and everyone who lived on Shaker Street called him Grandpa.

When Grandpa retired, he gave his old toolshed in the backyard to Michael. Now it was a clubhouse where Michael and his two best friends could create new things. They called it the Maker Shack.

"Want some help?" Grandpa Henry asked.

Michael knew that Grandpa could fix up the telescope in minutes. Truthfully, he'd probably make it even better. But that wasn't what Michael wanted. He was determined to solve this on his own.

"I'll figure it out," Michael told him.

"You're just like me when I was your age," Grandpa said with a chuckle. "Well, whippersnapper, come on upstairs. I'll give you a quiet place to think."

Grandpa pointed to the narrow steps at the end of the hallway. At the top of Michael's purple-painted Victorian house was a tower room with windows facing every direction. Grandpa Henry lived in that tower.

"Come along," Grandpa said. "I'll share my snack." He was carrying a small plate piled with cookies. Clearly, he'd been sneaking back from the kitchen when he'd found Michael.

"Yum," Michael said. "Thanks." He followed Grandpa up the stairs.

They sat in two super comfy overstuffed chairs that faced a big window. Grandpa Henry had his own telescope, and Michael stared at it while they ate the cookies.

The telescope was big, and Grandpa had made it himself. It was called a Galileo telescope.

He'd used two lenses. One was concave. That meant it was thinner at the center of the circular glass disc. The other was convex. The convex lens was thicker in the center and thinner at the edges. The two lenses were placed at opposite ends of a white plastic pipe.

It was a great telescope. Grandpa could see the stars clearly. Plus, he could see everything from their house, all the way to Liv's house at the bottom of Shaker Street.

Michael wasn't trying to make such a fancy telescope.

Liv's birthday was coming up, and he wanted to make her a present. She loved looking at the stars.

Actually, she liked to search the sky for alien life and UFOs. But since those didn't exist, Michael thought a telescope to look at stars would be the next best thing.

His little telescope wouldn't see much further than the moon, but it would be cool and he knew she'd love it.

Michael was staring at Grandpa's telescope when he realized that his grandfather had fallen asleep in his chair. His loud snore rattled through the room.

Smiling, Michael got up. He moved to a small empty table and set down the supplies for Liv's present.

Looking at Grandpa's telescope, he realized that the problem with Liv's was that there was no way to focus the lenses.

His weren't fancy concave and convex lenses. Instead, Michael had taken the simple lenses out of the two magnifying glasses. They looked like two clear glass discs.

Using tape, he'd secured one lens on one side of a cardboard tube and another lens on the other side.

With another long look at Grandpa Henry's amazing scope, he saw that there was a part that twisted, allowing the lenses to get closer together or further apart. That was how you focused the telescope.

*That's it,* Michael thought. *I need a way to move the lenses.*

He had an idea. He went to Grandpa Henry's bathroom and found an empty toilet paper tube. Using scissors, Michael cut the tube so it would fit inside the large cardboard tube he already had.

He slid the small tube into the bigger one. Then he taped one of the magnifying lenses to the end of that smaller tube.

He taped the other lens to the end of the big tube. Now the little tube could twist and move in and out.

"I think I fixed it!" Michael said. He took the telescope to the window that looked over Shaker Street and pointed it toward the sky.

Looking through the end with the smaller tube, he could now slide the tube and move the image around until things came clear. He saw the moon. He checked out a couple bright stars. Then he pointed the telescope down toward Shaker Street.

"What's that?" he muttered to himself. Michael twisted the lens around to get a clearer view.

There was a woman walking quickly in the light of the streetlamps. She was wearing a long, dark coat and dark hat.

If Michael wasn't using the telescope, he'd never have seen her.

He adjusted the telescope again, focusing on her arms.

She was carrying a rolled-up piece of paper, like a map or poster, and a shovel.

"Strange," Michael muttered to himself. He saw the woman look around, as if checking to make sure she wasn't being followed. After that, Michael saw her jump a fence into a neighbor's yard.

A few minutes later the figure came back. She appeared to be shaking her head sadly.

Michael stared out a few minutes more until the woman disappeared behind a large leafy tree near the house where Leo and his dad lived.

Michael set down the telescope.

"Strange things are happening on Shaker Street," he said to himself.

In the morning, he'd tell Leo what he saw.

Liv would come over.

And together, they would investigate.

# CHAPTER TWO

When Leo woke up, Michael was sitting in a chair near the bed, staring at him. "Tell Liv to come over for breakfast," he said in a rush. "I gotta show you both something."

Leo yawned. Then without asking what the hurry was, got out his laptop. It was old. Michael had rescued it before it was thrown away and fixed it up. The laptop worked great, most of the time.

Leo logged in. He asked Michael what was for breakfast, then he messaged Liv.

*LeoTheLion: Pancakes!*

*UFOWatcher: be there in 5*

"She's on the way," Leo reported. "Though I can't see how she'll get here in five minutes. Shaker Street is a huge hill." Leo often complained about going up and down the hill. "It would take me a lot longer," he said, pointing to himself. "Little legs. They're my curse."

Michael laughed. He was sure that Liv would be there fast. She always moved fast.

"I have a problem," Michael confessed to Leo. He wanted to solve this before Liv arrived.

"Telescope still busted?" Leo asked as he got dressed in a T-shirt and shorts.

"Nah," Michael said. "I figured that out." He got dressed quickly. "It's that I don't want to tell Liv about the telescope yet. I want it to be a surprise." Liv's birthday wasn't for four more days.

"Why's that a problem?" Leo said. "I can keep a secret. I won't tell her."

Michael picked up the telescope from his desk. "Last night, when I was checking to be sure the magnification worked, I saw —" He didn't finish saying what he'd seen because just then, the bedroom door slammed open with a heavy bang.

"It's a new speed record. Four minutes, fifty-three seconds," Liv exclaimed as she crashed into the room and flopped onto Michael's lower bunk bed. "I told you I could be here in five minutes. I ran the whole way."

How TO...

Her cheeks were red, same as her glasses frames. In fact, everything Liv was wearing was red. Her shirt, leggings, and shoes — they were all slightly different shades of red.

"What's with the red?" Michael asked her as he stuffed the telescope behind his back. He knew that if he told her about the suspicious woman, he'd have to explain how he saw her. That meant showing Liv the telescope.

"I'm dressed for the mystery," Liv explained, rolling on her side. She propped herself on Leo's pillow. "There's something strange happening on Shaker Street. We have to investigate."

Michael was so surprised, he nearly dropped the telescope. "I know!" he said. "I was going to tell you the same thing!"

He wasn't sure what Liv's red clothes had to do with the mysterious woman he'd seen. He'd have to ask. But first, Michael wanted to know, "How'd you find out?"

"Everyone's talking about it," Liv said. She scooted off the bed. "The news is all over Shaker Street."

"I feel like I am missing something big here," Leo told Michael and Liv. "What are you two talking about?"

"I was about to tell you when Liv came in," Michael explained. "Last night, I was in Grandpa's tower room. I saw something odd."

He decided to show Liv her present. It would make explaining so much easier. "Here. I made this for your birthday," he said, holding out the telescope.

She squinted and asked, "Uh, what is it?"

Michael sighed and explained, "A telescope. You can use it to look at the stars."

"AWESOME!" Liv cheered. "Thanks Michael!"

"I offered to help," Leo said. "Michael said no, but still, I offered." Leo hadn't made Liv anything yet. But he had a few ideas.

"Thanks to you too!" Liv said, smiling. "It's perfect. And we can use it to solve the mystery!"

She hurried to the window and looked out. Michael showed her how to adjust the focus, twisting the inner tube until the image became clear.

"Point it toward the street," Michael said when he noticed that Liv was looking up at the sky. "I saw the woman down there." He pointed to the sidewalk.

"What woman?" Liv asked.

"The mysterious one," he said. "The woman who was sneaking around Shaker Street in the dark." At Liv's blank stare, Michael added, "I thought we were going to investigate who she is and what she was doing."

"I don't know anything about a woman," Liv said, shaking her head.

"But you said there was something suspicious," Michael countered.

"Yes. There is something strange going on," Liv began. "And we need to help Sheriff Kawasaki investigate."

Liv always believed that the sheriff wanted her, Leo, and Michael to help solve mysteries. The boys weren't so sure, but Liv was confident the sheriff needed them.

Leo looked from Michael to Liv and back again. "You two are so confusing!" he shouted. He raised his hands in frustration. "Will someone explain what's going on? Please!"

"It's the holes," Liv said. She sounded irritated, as if they should have known. "At nine different houses on Shaker Street, people woke up today and found strange holes all over their yards. Big holes. Little holes. Front yards. Backyards. Holes are everywhere. It's so weird."

"That *is* weird," Leo said. "I wonder if there are holes in my yard?"

Leo and his dad rented a whole floor of a Victorian house about halfway down Shaker Street. That was the last place Michael had seen the woman.

"I don't know which nine houses they were at. But, there were a lot of holes in my yard," Liv reported. "I think the aliens may have hidden hundreds of energy capsules on Shaker Street while we all slept last night."

Leo was still confused, and now, Michael was completely baffled. "What are you talking about?" Michael asked Liv. "Aliens? Energy capsules?"

"The holes, of course," Liv said, as if that cleared everything up. "The aliens' holes. I know the aliens will come back soon. When the spaceship arrives, I want to be ready to greet them." She went on, "I'm wearing red because these aliens are from Mars. Martians live on a red planet, you know?"

"Yes . . . ," Michael said, uncertain what that had to do with anything. Liv kept talking, but nothing she said made sense to him.

Liv explained, "The energy capsules are necessary to power their ships to get back to Mars after the aliens take over the Earth. They are storing the capsules here for the Martian invasion."

"What are you talking about?" Michael asked again, his voice rising. "There are no aliens on Mars. Scientists have sent a rover there. They have photos."

"Did they look everywhere? The whole planet?" Liv said, putting her hands on her hips. She didn't wait for Michael to answer. "The Martians are sneaky. They like to hide."

"You're wearing red because they call it the red planet?" Leo asked, raising one eyebrow. "Uh, Liv, Mars is red because the surface of the planet is covered with an iron dust. They sky looks red when the dust is swept into the atmosphere."

"I know all that!" Then she said, "Red. It's a happy color. They'll be happy when they see me all dressed in red." She straightened her shirt. "The Martians don't want to go to war. They want to stop our astronauts from coming there, building new neighborhoods, and putting up fast-food restaurants." She frowned. "I am going to explain everything to them. We aren't planning to send them chicken nuggets. We want to live in harmony."

There was a tiny bit of truth in what Liv was saying. Michael knew scientists talked about colonizing Mars. They'd even found signs of water on the planet.

But no one on Earth had the technology to send people there. For sure, no one was planning to build a restaurant on Mars. So far it was a fantasy.

"Liv, you've got to stop listening to alien-invader podcasts," Michael said. Liv loved listening to podcasts that talked about aliens, Bigfoot, ghosts, and other supernatural creatures. "There are no Martians on Mars," Michael assured her.

"Then explain the holes," Liv challenged. She looked out the window with her new telescope.

"The woman I saw last night was carrying a large piece of paper and a shovel," Michael said. "I think she was digging the holes."

"Maybe she's an alien?" Liv suggested.

"I don't think so," Michael told her. "She looked pretty normal to me, except that she was sneaking around."

"Did you see her face?" Liv asked.

"No," Michael admitted.

"How many arms did she have?" Liv asked.

"I'm pretty sure it was two," Michael replied.

"But you aren't certain, are you?" Liv challenged.

The question was so ridiculous, Michael didn't answer.

"All this Martian talk is freaking me out," Leo said. "I think I hear my dad calling. I should go home."

"He's out of town," Michael reminded Leo. "You're staying here for the weekend, remember?"

"Bummer." Leo sighed.

"Let's go check out the alien holes," Liv told Michael.

"There might even be some right here in your yard!" she added. "If there are holes at nine houses on Shaker Street, yours could definitely be one of them."

Michael hadn't seen the woman by his house, but he hadn't been watching all night. "I guess it's possible the woman was here," he admitted.

"I think we should stay inside today," Leo told the others. "Let the sheriff check out the aliens." He rubbed his belly. "The idea of Martians on Shaker Street makes me feel a little sick."

Liv grabbed his arm. "You're just hungry," she told Leo, pulling him out of the room. "Let's have some pancakes. Then we can go on an exploring adventure. The aliens left a big mess out there."

"Messy Martians . . . ," Leo moaned as he followed Liv into the hallway.

Michael took Liv's telescope and looked out the window. Now that it was light, he could see a lot of holes in yards up and down the street. He didn't know what they meant. Or who'd made them. Or why.

And yet, Michael knew one important thing.

"There are no aliens on Shaker Street," he said confidently.

But no one heard him.

Liv and Leo were already downstairs having breakfast, getting ready for the day.

# CHAPTER THREE

After breakfast, Leo and Liv followed Michael through the purple gate at the side of his house and into the backyard.

Michael was surprised to find that there were, in fact, several holes in his yard.

They were small, about the size of baseballs. They seemed randomly placed around the yard. It was as if whoever made them had been in a huge hurry to dig as many holes as fast as possible.

The grass was patchy in the spots that had been dug under. The ground was turned over, then packed back on top.

Leo reported, "There are six holes between the big tree and the door to the Maker Shack."

"Six buried energy capsules," Liv said, stopping at the one closest to them all. She looked up at Michael. "Sorry about your grass. When I talk to the aliens, I'll ask them about cleaning up Shaker Street. They should have been more careful."

"Messy Martians," Leo muttered, shaking his head.

Michael came to stand next to Liv by a hole. Leo held back, a little behind the two of them. He peeked over Liv's shoulder.

"We shouldn't get too close," he said. "There might be radiation."

"The podcast said the Martians are environmentally friendly," Liv said. "They use metal compounds to make energy cells instead of gas and oil and coal, like us."

She squatted down for a closer look at the hole. "Their technology is ahead of us in so many ways," she added. "When we're friends, we can share resources."

"If I find an energy capsule, I'll believe you," Michael said. He bent down next to Liv and using his hands, dug out the loose dirt in the hole.

"Careful," Leo warned. "I think it's a bad idea to touch Martian holes."

"I think these might be from rabbits," Michael said. He quickly found the bottom of the hole. It wasn't very deep. "Rabbits dig holes."

"There are other animals that dig too," Leo said, coming forward and sitting on the ground next to Michael and Liv. "Chipmunks, squirrels, skunks . . ."

"Skunks?" Liv asked. "No way. There are too many holes." She shook her head. "It would have taken a million skunks to make so many holes all at one time."

Michael bit his bottom lip. "Okay, so maybe these aren't animal holes," he said.

"Bummer," Leo said. He looked up to the clear sky. "Let's go in the Maker Shack where it's safe. I don't want to be out here, just in case the aliens come back." He had his laptop with him. "I'll check the news and see what the neighbors are saying about the holes."

The three of them entered the clubhouse. Michael pushed carefully on the door in case Grandpa Henry had booby-trapped it.

He did that sometimes. Actually, he did that a lot.

The door opened. Nothing happened.

"We're clear," Michael reported, stepping inside. The others followed.

Leo's computer desk was made out of a piece of wood on two piles of bricks. He set down his computer and got to work. "I'll let you know what I find out," he said.

"I wonder if anyone saw the spaceship?" Liv said. She went to read articles with Leo on the computer.

Michael got to work too. "If we're going to investigate the neighborhood, we need a few things," he said.

There was a long workbench in the center of the shack. It was made of an old door sitting on top of fruit crates.

All around the workbench, the walls of the Maker Shack were lined with tall shelves. There were bins and boxes full of the things Michael, Liv, and Leo needed for projects.

On the wall were the Maker Shack rules. A cardboard sign said:

The Mysterious Makers
of Shaker Street Promise

**1) We turn old things into new things.**

**2) We don't use new things if we can use old things.**

Leo had scribbled at the bottom:

**Computers are okay.**

Liv had added:

**Phones are okay if zombies attack. Call me!**

The last line read:

**This contract is legally binding.**

Michael set the Maker Sack on the bench. It was an old blue backpack that he'd found in the school trash. Liv had fixed it up with duct tape and written *Maker Sack* on the front in silver tape strips. He was about to load it with supplies for the day.

"Where did I put my calculator?" Michael mumbled as he searched through labeled bins. None of them actually said *Calculator.* There was one that said *School Supplies* on the side. The calculator wasn't in it.

He moved down the row of shelves and pulled down a plastic tub that said *Random Things* on the label. Pushing the lid off, Michael began to look through loose items. He found dice, spoons, broken wind chimes, and some playing cards.

While he searched for the calculator, Liv and Leo read about the holes.

"Sheriff Kawasaki said her officers are investigating," Leo read from the *Shaker Street News* website.

"She needs us," Liv commented. "We better hurry." She looked over at Michael and asked, "Are you ready?"

"I can't find a calculator," Michael replied. He took a dog collar out of the box of random things.

"It's not in there," Liv told him. "I put it in a small box marked *HELLO*."

"Huh?" Leo turned to Liv. Then he paused, and a slow smile spread across his face. "Oh, that's kinda clever."

Liv explained to Michael as he went to get that box, "There are all kinds of words you can make on a calculator. *Hello* is probably the most popular one. You type in 0.7734, then flip it over to read HELLO."

Leo laughed. "Did you know that spelling on a calculator is called beghilos, because those are the most frequently used numbers? I mean, numbers that can look like letters, on a calculator."

"I didn't know —" Liv started when Michael interrupted.

"Found it!" Michael took down the box. There was only one thing inside: the calculator that he'd found in the park. It had the name *RANDY* written in pen on it. Liv had made *LOST CALCULATOR* posters, but no one ever called them.

"We'll use Randy's calculator to solve this mystery!" Michael said, setting it in the middle of the workbench. "If we ever meet him, we can say thanks."

"Want to hear a calculator joke?" Leo asked Michael and Liv.

"Sure," Michael said, turning on the calculator to make sure it worked.

"Why did the horse stay inside the barn?" Leo asked his friends.

"I don't know," Liv said.

"Why?" Michael asked.

Leo told him to start doing the math on the calculator. "Take 26 times 1,000. Then add 500. Then add 45. Take away 23. Multiply the answer by 2. Add 1," Leo said. "Now, turn the calculator upside down."

Michael turned it over to see the word they'd made.

Leo prompted the answer. "The horse couldn't leave the barn because he didn't have any . . ."

"SHOES," Michael read the calculator's numbers as words. He and Liv chuckled.

"Calculators are funny," Liv told Leo. Then she asked Michael, "What do you need it for?"

"A metal detector," Michael told her. "You said the aliens used metal for their rocket energy. I figure if we can find a buried energy cell, then we will have proof of the Martians."

"So you believe Liv?" Leo said. "I never thought I'd see the day when Michael Wilson admitted he believed in aliens."

Michael smiled. "When we don't find any metal alien energy cells, then we'll know that woman I saw through the telescope was digging the holes. We'll go find her."

"That's more like it," Leo told Michael. "I was worried you were turning into Liv."

"There's only one Liv Hernandez," Liv said proudly. "That's me."

Michael chuckled as he got the other two things he needed: duct tape and an old AM radio.

"I bet the aliens dug extra holes to confuse us," Liv said as she came to stand by Michael. "We have to figure out where they hid the energy cells. How can I help?"

"Hold the calculator," Michael told her. He turned on the radio and set it to the highest number station on the AM band. Static echoed through the Maker Shack. He turned the volume to max.

Michael put the radio against the back of the calculator. "Move the calculator around slowly until there is a beeping noise," Michael told her.

When beeping started, Liv took the tape and attached the calculator to the radio.

"Done," Michael said, holding up the metal detector.

"Does it work?" Liv asked.

"Let's check," Michael said. He got a silver spoon from the box of random things and set it on the workbench. When he hovered the metal detector close to the spoon, the machine beeped.

"I don't get it," Leo said, turning around. "It's just a radio taped to a calculator."

"The radio waves from the calculator bounce off the metal spoon. We can hear the sound through the AM radio," Michael explained.

Liv announced. "Let's go try detecting stuff in the yard!"

Michael put the metal detector and some extra duct tape in the Maker Sack.

Liv and Michael headed toward the door.

"Hang on," Leo told them. He was still at the computer. "I just found something interesting online."

"What is it?" Liv asked. She and Michael stood behind Leo's desk.

Leo played a video on his laptop.

On the newscast, a middle-aged woman with wild blond hair was standing in her backyard. She was wearing a bathrobe and fuzzy slippers. The kids all recognized Tilly Thorne. She taught kindergarten at their school.

Mrs. Thorne pointed to the holes and then looked into the camera. "The aliens were right here!" she announced. "There were a few of them. All wandering around the street. I locked my doors — fast — and hid."

"What exactly did you see?" the reporter asked Mrs. Thorne. "Can you describe the aliens?"

"I just got a good look at one of the creatures," Mrs. Thorne reported. "It was tall, thin, wearing a dark alien cloak and moving slow like a shadow." She touched her forehead. "And it had a light in the middle of its skull."

# CHAPTER FOUR

"I'm not going anywhere," Leo announced, turning off the computer. "It's too dangerous out there."

"We have to make contact!" Liv countered. "Our government is going to come to Shaker Street because of the holes. I have to be there when they arrive. The Martians need me to help with the peace negotiations."

“You’re crazy,” Leo told her. “The Martians don’t need you. They would want to work with professionals who know all about aliens.”

“I’m a professional!” Liv replied, putting her hands on her hips.

Michael half listened to Liv and Leo talk about aliens. He pulled down several boxes and found a few additional supplies.

Opening the Maker Sack, he threw a long piece of elastic, some safety pins, and a small flashlight into the bag.

Then he added extra duct tape and the metal detector.

When Michael was ready, he turned to Liv and Leo. "Let's go," he said.

"Cool." Liv was right behind Michael.

Leo took a little longer to log off and shut down his computer. He liked to complain about danger, but Michael knew he'd come along. Leo wouldn't miss an adventure.

They started in Michael's yard. He took out the metal detector and handed it to Liv. She held it over each hole and they listened for beeps.

"There's nothing metal here," Liv reported once they'd explored all the holes in Michael's yard.

"Maybe the energy cells aren't metal?" Leo suggested.

"The podcast had these Mars experts on it. They were positive that the fuel cells are metal," Liv said. "Clearly, there just aren't any cells here. We need to go to Mrs. Thorne's house." She opened the back gate to Michael's yard. "She saw the aliens."

Michael didn't argue with her. When Liv was convinced of something, it was impossible to change her mind. He'd have to prove to her that it was the woman he'd seen who was digging holes. And to do that, he needed facts.

"Okay, let's go," Michael said. He would search for clues while they walked down Shaker Street.

Leo found the first clue. There was a trail of muddy footprints fanning out in many directions. It looked like there had been a lot of different shoes that made the prints.

"I'm going to check these out," Michael said, picking one set to follow.

Liv and Leo waited.

The footprints went from the front of Michael's house into the yard next door. Then, they came out of the yard next door and back onto the sidewalk.

When he came back, Michael said, "Those are not alien footprints."

"Maybe someone was out walking their dog," Leo suggested. "The footprints could be anyone's."

Liv pointed to prints that went other directions. She reminded them, "Mrs. Thorne said there were many invaders."

Michael took a good look at the closest prints.

"This marking is about the same size as my tennis shoe," he said. Michael had big feet for a ten year old. "It has ridges like my tennis shoe too." He looked at Liv and asked, "Do aliens wear tennis shoes?"

"Maybe," Liv replied, seriously considering it. "I'll ask them when they come back."

"We need more clues," Michael said as they continued down the sidewalk.

Mrs. Thorne's house was a few houses further, but before they got there, a door to a bright green house swung open. A small voice called out, "Liv! Michael! Leo!"

It was CoCo, Liv's five-year-old sister. She came running out of the house and toward them. CoCo was wearing a long brown coat and a hat that was way too big for her.

In one hand she had a magnifying glass like the one Michael used to make the telescope. In her other hand was a notebook.

"I'm a detective," CoCo told them, skidding to a stop near Liv. "I'm investigating."

"We're investigating too," Liv told her sister. "Tell us what you discovered."

"Shhh," CoCo whispered as she leaned in. She looked up and down the street as if she was about to share a major secret. Pointing over her shoulder, she admitted, "I've only been to one house. Mom said I couldn't talk to strangers."

Liv explained, "That's where CoCo's best friend, Hassan, lives."

CoCo flipped open her notebook. She read her report in her detective voice.

"Here are the facts: Hassan's mom didn't see anything strange," she said. "His dad didn't see anything either. Hassan was asleep all night." She shut the notebook.

"Too bad," Liv said with a frown. She looked at the house and the front yard. There were no obvious holes. "Are there holes in the back?"

"Yes," CoCo said, "but they don't know who made them."

"I guess that's all," Leo said. He was ready to move on and put his mind at ease for good. "There's nothing new here." He swept the back of his hand across his forehead. "Whew. No aliens. That's good."

Liv said, "We'll go to Mrs. Thorne's house now. It seems like she might be the only one who has a clue about the holes."

"Oh. Clues? You wanted to know about clues?" CoCo opened her notebook again. "I thought you only wanted facts."

"Aren't they pretty much the same?" Leo whispered to Michael. Michael shrugged.

"You're supposed to be the detective," Liv told her sister. "Isn't finding clues an important part of the job?"

"I get confused. I keep forgetting what I am supposed to do," CoCo admitted. "Want to see what Hassan found near one of the holes?"

"Yes!" Michael said, leaping forward.

"Was it an energy cell?" Liv asked eagerly.

"It's alien money," CoCo told them.

Leo said, "I don't know what I expected, but that wasn't it."

"Hassan said I could have a coin. He found a lot of them." CoCo read from her notebook. "They weren't in an alien's hole, but they were buried near one." She smiled. "Hassan was outside playing aliens and digging more holes. That's how he found the coins."

"Good detective work," Liv told her.

CoCo smiled. She shut the notebook again and reached into her pocket. When she opened her palm, she was holding a small silver disc. It was worn down on the sides, and the markings were mostly faded.

"Can I look closer?" Michael asked.

"Don't lose it," CoCo warned. "It's mine."

"I'll be careful. I promise," Michael said. He held the disc between his fingers. CoCo was right. It was a coin.

He handed the coin to Leo. "Ever seen anything like this?" he asked.

"It's a coin," Leo confirmed. He rubbed it on his T-shirt, then stared harder at it. "It says 1717. And has maybe a cross or crossed anchors on it." Leo shook his head. "I'm not sure."

"What does 1717 mean?" Michael asked Leo. "Anything historically important happen then?"

"I wish I had my computer," Leo said. He asked Liv, "Do you have your phone?"

"I left it in the Shack," Liv reported. She turned to Michael. "It's weird that the aliens left coins in Hassan's yard, right?"

"Aliens didn't leave this," Michael said, taking the coin back from Leo.

He handed it to CoCo. "I think this belongs to someone else," he told her. "You can keep it for now, but you might have to return it later. It's very old and probably very valuable."

"But Hassan found ten!" CoCo protested. "All I got was one."

"If we find out who they belong to, Hassan will have to give his back too," Michael said.

CoCo sighed. "Okay. I'll take good care of it," she said. She looked down the street. Liv could see their mom standing outside on the sidewalk. "I told Mom I'd be right back. I better go." She hurried away.

"Running must be a family thing," Leo remarked, noting how fast CoCo got to her own house. "CoCo and Liv are the fastest sisters on Shaker Street."

Liv laughed. Then she asked Michael, "What do you think about the coin?"

"I don't know yet," he said.

Michael was thinking about 1717 while they walked the rest of the way to Mrs. Thorne's house. *Where did that coin come from?* he wondered. *And how did it end up in Hassan's yard?*

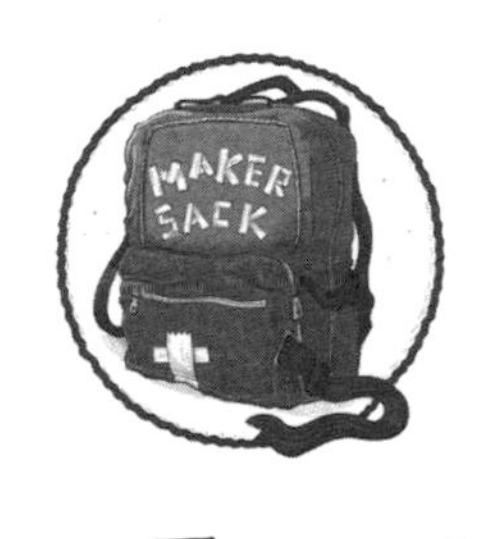


# CHAPTER FIVE

Mrs. Thorne wasn't home. There was a note taped to her front door that read *Go Away, Aliens!*

"What should we do?" Leo asked. "Maybe we should go away too?"

"We can't leave," Liv told him. "We have to find out what the aliens looked like. Mrs. Thorne is our only witness!"

“Bah,” Leo complained as he sat down on the top porch step.

Michael slipped off the Maker Sack’s straps. He reached in the bag and pulled out the metal detector. He set that to the side.

Leo was sitting next to Michael. He picked up the metal detector.

“If there are any more coins in Hassan’s yard, we could use this to find them.” Leo turned it on and swept the metal detector around Mrs. Thorne’s porch. The AM radio hummed quietly. “No hidden treasure here,” Leo reported.

Michael emptied the rest of his supplies onto the porch. He said to Liv, “Can you help me with a Maker project?”

“Sure,” Liv said.

“What about me?” Leo asked.

"You're part of the project," Michael told him. He raised the elastic band and said to Leo, "Lean forward."

"No. Wait. What? Why?" Leo asked. "What is going on?" He set the metal detector on the porch.

"I want to try something," Michael said.

"Okay," Leo said. He leaned forward.

"I'm making a headband for you," Michael said.

"Oh, cool," Leo said. "I'll be like a rock-and-roll king."

"More like a miner," Michael said. "Or someone camping."

"I'd rather be a rock-and-roll king," Leo said. He pinched his lips together. "Camping involves hiking and mining is too dirty."

"Stay still," Liv told Leo.

"You're just trying to get me to stop talking," Leo said.

"Maybe," Liv admitted with a smile.

Michael measured the elastic around Leo's head. Liv helped safety pin it to the right size. The band was tight. At the front, right in the center of Leo's forehead, Michael attached the small flashlight. He taped it with a lot of duct tape so it wouldn't fall off.

"This is awesome," Leo said when Michael turned on the light. "I can see without using my hands to hold anything."

"Exactly," Michael said. "I think that's how the mystery woman managed to shovel all those holes while holding that big paper. She was wearing something like this on her forehead."

MAKER
SACK

Leo said, "That would make sense. Mrs. Thorne said the Martian had a light in its forehead."

"Interesting," Liv said, considering it. "You know, Martians don't need lights. I read in *Suspicious Surprises* magazine that they can see in the dark."

"How would anyone know that?" Leo asked.

"Martians have been to Earth before," Liv told him. "Lots of people have seen them."

Michael still didn't think Mrs. Thorne had seen an actual Martian. He said, "I think we should ask Mrs. Thorne for more details about what she witnessed."

They all agreed to wait for their neighbor.

# CHAPTER SIX

Half an hour later, Liv, Leo, and Michael were still sitting on the porch. Mrs. Thorne hadn't come back.

Leo was still wearing the light on his head. They were playing I Spy. Leo would think of something he could see. Liv and Michael would guess. And then Leo would reveal the answer by turning on the flashlight and pointing his head at whatever it was he'd been looking at.

It was hard to see the flashlight beam in the sunlight, and sometimes Leo would have to try a few times before they guessed. The game was fun, but they weren't learning anything more about the holes.

"Let's walk around," Liv suggested. "We can explore with the metal detector while we wait."

"Great idea," Michael said. He got up and turned the detector on. They walked a few doors down to Leo's house. There were five holes in the front yard and eight more in the back.

"Thirteen holes," Leo said. "That's a lot."

Michael turned on the metal detector. Very slowly, he and Liv and Leo wandered from hole to hole, listening to the radio buzz. There was nothing in the first twelve holes.

Then suddenly the metal detector began to beep. They were near the thirteenth hole, but not over the top of it. It was just like CoCo had described the hole and coins at Hassan's house.

Michael wished he had a shovel. Instead, he dug with his hands, as deep as he could. Leo held the detector. It was beeping loud and fast.

"There's something down here!" Michael reported as his fingers touched an old, dirty canvas bag. He pulled it out of the ground. "Look!"

Inside the small, frayed bag were several of the same type of coins that Hassan had found. There were also some odd bones and several pieces of colored glass. All the items had been carefully wrapped.

"I don't think these things belong to the aliens," Liv said. "I think they are someone's treasure. We shouldn't mess around with it."

"Are you admitting that aliens didn't dig the holes?" Michael asked her.

"That would be good news," Leo said. "No aliens!"

"I'm not saying that," Liv told them both. "I just don't think *this* little baggie belongs to the Martians."

"I agree," Michael said happily. "We need to find out who it does belong to." He put the canvas sack in the Maker Sack. "Should we explore other yards?" he asked his friends.

"No," Leo said, glancing to Mrs. Thorne's house. "I think Mrs. Thorne is home."

There was a woman walking slowly by the house, but she didn't stop.

"Oh, my mistake," Leo said. "That's obviously not her."

The woman was tall and thin and looked familiar to Michael.

"I think that might be the woman I saw last night," Michael said. "She's wearing a different coat, so I can't be sure. But —" He turned to Liv. "Do you have the telescope?"

"I left it at the Maker Shack with my phone," Liv told him.

"We need to make another Maker Sack," Leo said. "So Liv can carry all her stuff around too."

"Good idea. I'll start looking in garbage cans for an old tote bag or backpack," Michael said. Changing the subject, he stepped forward. "I think we should go talk to that woman."

"On it," Liv, being the fastest, took off toward the woman. Like usual, Liv was speedy, but the woman began to run.

"Hey wait!" Liv called out. "We want to talk to you!"

"No!" the woman called back.

She was much quicker than Liv. Near the top of the street, she disappeared between two thick trees.

Liv waited by one of those trees for Michael and Leo to catch up.

"I lost her," Liv said, huffing hard.

"That was so strange!" Michael exclaimed, looking in the direction the woman had disappeared. She could have gone anywhere in those thick trees. "Why would she run away?" he wondered.

"Maybe she's an alien," Leo said. "If so, I'm glad we didn't catch her!"

"She's not an alien," Liv told Leo. "She was just a regular woman."

"How do you know?" Michael asked, even though he was happy that Liv was agreeing with him now.

"I know what aliens are like. Plus, she dropped a piece of paper," Liv reported. "Aliens don't use paper."

She bent down between the two trees and picked up an antique-looking page. It was about the size of the notebook paper they used in school. But it had a jagged edge. This was a torn part of something much larger.

"I think that's part of the paper I saw her carrying last night," Michael said.

"Look. It's a map of Shaker Street," Liv reported. "It's just part of it, but that's for sure what it is."

"Really?" Michael asked. He leaned in to look.

Sure enough, it was an antique map of the street. None of the houses had been built yet. It looked like the street was a hilly part of an old farm. There were a couple big areas marked with thick black lines, but Michael didn't know why.

"I wonder who owned the farm?" Michael muttered to himself.

Leo overheard and said, "I'll check it out online when we get back to the Maker Shack." He took the paper. He ran a finger over it. He smelled it. Then, to everyone's surprise, he licked the corner of the page.

"There's more here," Leo said at last. "There's something else on the map written in disappearing ink." He put his hands on his hips and announced, "Luckily, I know how to find out what it says!"

# CHAPTER SEVEN

"I'll need a light bulb," Leo told Michael when they got back to the Maker Shack.

Liv found one in a bin.

Leo frowned. "I guess I should have also said that I needed a lamp to put it in."

Michael had to run back to the house. He brought the small table lamp from his bedroom.

Leo put the bulb in the lamp and set the lampshade on the table. "We don't need the shade," he said. "But we need the light bulb to get hot."

There was no way to speed up the heat of the bulb. They just had to wait.

"Are you sure you know what you're doing?" Liv asked Leo. "Because I don't have any clue!"

"A thousand percent," Leo confirmed. "Trust me."

While they waited for the bulb to get hot, Liv sat at Leo's computer and typed in *1717*. It was the year printed on the old coin Hassan had found.

The first thing that popped up was a list of important things that had happened that year.

Liv read a few of them out loud. "In January, Count Carl Gyllenborg was arrested. He planned to assassinate a royal guy named James Stuart."

"Hmmm," Michael said. "Interesting but probably not what we need. What else?"

While she looked, Michael and Leo checked the bulb. It was really warm, but not quite hot.

"Oh!" Liv bounced up out of Leo's plastic desk chair. "Here's something about treasure."

"Read it," Michael said.

Liv read, "In 1717, the British pirate known as Blackbeard captured a ship called *La Concorde*. He changed the name to *Queen Anne's Revenge*."

"Pirates are better than aliens," Leo said.

"Blackbeard's real name was Edward Teach," Leo said, adding a fact he knew. "He got his nickname because of his dark beard."

Liv went on. "Blackbeard sent the slaves and the crew off the ship, but kept the treasure. He used the ship to attack other ships in the Caribbean," she said. "His treasure kept growing. Then in 1718, the ship ran into a sandbar in North Carolina. Some historians think he had plenty of time to hide his treasure. Others have been searching a sunken ship they found deep in the sea, hoping to find Blackbeard's treasure."

"Is the ship they found the *Queen Anne's Revenge*?" Michael asked.

"No one knows for sure. Maybe. Maybe not." Liv turned away from the computer. "How cool would it be if the coins we have are from Blackbeard's treasure?"

"It might make sense," Michael said, considering. "The coins could have been on *La Concorde.*"

"Or from another ship he raided," Leo added.

Michael pulled the small treasure sack out of the Maker Sack. "But what does Blackbeard's treasure have to do with the holes on Shaker Street?" He stared at the coins. "This is so weird."

"The map will tell us everything," Leo said, waving the paper they'd found. "I've used disappearing ink before. It's best when you make it with lemon juice."

"That's why you licked the paper," Liv said. "I thought you were just being gross."

"I wanted to see if it was lemony," Leo said proudly.

He added, "Even after so many years, it still tastes a little. To make a message from lemon juice writing reappear, you have to heat it up."

Leo held the page near the light bulb. He moved the page back and forth over the light bulb until the entire paper was warm. The heat of the bulb brought out the writing made in lemon juice.

The map piece they had was of the top of Shaker Street. But now, there were Xs all over the area.

"There's the spot my house was built," Michael said, pointing. "Why are there Xs all over the yard?"

"I think," Leo explained, "Xs mark where treasure is buried."

"You're a genius!" Michael cheered.

He looked closer at the map, then out the window. "Wow, whoever dug the holes missed every single X," Michael concluded.

"It's like they dug in the right areas, but since they didn't have the hidden part of the map, they missed all the coins," Leo said.

"You guys think the coins we have are someone's treasure?" Liv asked. "Whose?"

"Blackbeard the Pirate!" both Leo and Michael shouted at once.

"So let me get this straight," Liv said. She started pacing around the Maker Shack. "Little sacks of Blackbeard's treasure are hidden near the alien holes on Shaker Street?"

"Yes. But the holes aren't ali—" Michael began.

Leo put his hand out to stop Michael saying anymore. "You'll never convince her," he whispered. "Let's show her instead."

Leo opened a search engine on the laptop and typed in *History of Shaker Street*.

He'd barely even started reading, when he jumped up, pointing at the screen. "Blackbeard was here!"

"For sure?" Michael asked. "I thought no one knew what happened to him."

"Or where the treasure went," Liv added.

"They don't." Leo changed the way he said it. "Blackbeard *might* have been here. Some historians think he was the man who owned this big farm." He waved his hands around the room. "Before the houses were built, and it became Shaker Street!"

"That would mean the coins Hassan found might actually be Blackbeard's treasure," Michael said thoughtfully. "It's like being part of history! We need to find out who this map belongs to," he said. "I bet the treasure is hers."

"Maybe she doesn't want it back?" Leo said. "We could sell the treasure and buy a new laptop!"

Liv and Michael ignored him.

"How are we going to find the woman?" Liv said. "She ran away from me." Closing her eyes, she added, "She might be a thief."

"We need to find her and ask her what she was doing last night on Shaker Street. I have an idea," Michael said. "Remember how we tried to give Randy back his calculator?"

"We hung lost and found posters all over Shaker Street," Leo said. "But he never called us."

"But pirate treasure is better than a plastic calculator," Liv said. "Let's hang posters. I bet she'll call."

# CHAPTER EIGHT

**Lost Treasure?**

**Contact the Makers of Shaker Street**

The posters were simple and to the point. At the bottom was Liv's phone number, since she was the only one with a cell phone.

Michael, Leo, and Liv spent an hour putting up the flyers, then went to the Maker Shack to hang out.

"I think we should go dig up the treasure that is on this map," Leo said. "We can use the metal detector to find it."

"It's not ours," Michael said.

"Bummer," Leo said.

The phone rang.

"Hello?" Liv answered. Then, "Hi, CoCo. No, we haven't found out who the treasure belongs to." Pause. "And yes, you'll have to give back the old coin." She hung up.

"I guess the word's out," Michael said. "I wonder if everyone on Shaker Street is trying to dig up Blackbeard's Treasure."

Before Liv or Leo replied, the door to the Maker Shack swung open with a bang. Standing in the late afternoon light was a woman with long black hair and brown eyes. She was wearing pants and a sweater.

It was the same woman Michael had seen through the telescope. The same woman Liv had chased earlier. There were a whole lot of people with her. Some kids, some adults.

"We saw your poster. Do you have the treasure?" she asked.

"Just a few coins," Michael admitted.

She thought about that, then said, "Maybe you can help us," the woman said. She stepped inside the shack. The others followed.

Michael counted quickly. There were twenty people now stuffed in his shack, not counting him and Liv and Leo.

Michael could see that the woman was upset. "Maybe you should sit down," he said.

The woman chose Liv's beanbag chair.

Because she was tall, she tucked her legs underneath her and curled up into the chair.

"My name is Elizabeth Teach," she told them with a sniffle. Liv handed her a tissue.

"Edward Teach was Blackbeard the Pirate," Leo said. "Are you related?"

"Yes," she admitted. She pointed at the people in the room. "We're his descendants."

Elizabeth Teach pushed her hair back and said, "We have a family reunion every year. We get together and tell stories of Blackbeard." She raised her eyebrows. "My house was the first one built on Shaker Street. It dates back to the original farm. We were all cleaning up some junk in the attic, and we found this old map behind a loose board. Can you believe it's been hidden there all this time?"

Liv said, "That's terrific." Michael and Leo agreed.

"I'm certain it's a map to Blackbeard's treasure," Elizabeth said, standing up. "But we can't read it. There are nine big areas that are blocked out, but there are no markings for where the treasure is buried. Family legend says he packed it into small bags and hid them all separately. There might even be hundreds of buried bags."

Leo showed her the one they'd found. "Like this?" he asked.

"Exactly," Elizabeth confirmed excitedly. "When we found the map, we started talking about the community center we'd build with the money. We were so excited, we decided to head out and search, even though it was dark."

She took the bag from Leo. “So, last night, we dug holes in the nine areas marked on the map.”

Michael had only seen the woman in the dark, but now he knew Mrs. Thorne was right. There were a lot of people digging up yards on Shaker Street last night. *People,* he thought, *not aliens.*

“Digging holes without a plan wasn’t a very good idea,” one of the young cousins said from a spot near Leo’s computer table. “We just made a mess and didn’t find anything.”

Elizabeth said, “Mrs. Thorne saw me with my headlamp on. She called the sheriff. The sheriff called the TV news.” She scratched her head. “Anyway, we’re desperate to get our treasure back.” She set the lost-and-found flyer on the workbench. “Can you help us?”

“Yes,” Michael nodded. “We can.”

# CHAPTER NINE

Elizabeth Teach gave Michael, Liv, and Leo the full map of Shaker Street. They reattached the torn corner they'd found with some tape.

Leo showed the family how to bring out the markings by using the lamp's heat.

Michael showed them how the metal detector worked.

"We thought about using a metal detector," Elizabeth Teach told them. "But since it was so late, no stores were open. We couldn't buy one." She looked at Michael's invention. "I wish we'd thought to make one. That would have been helpful."

"We make everything we need," Michael told her. "Next time you need something, you can ask us." He smiled.

Leo had a big question. "Why hasn't anyone on Shaker Street found treasure before now?" he wondered as they got ready to go out. "I mean you have to dig to build a house. Or a garden. In all these years, someone should have found some treasure."

"It's a good question," Michael said, wondering what the answer might be.

"I know," Liv said. "It's the Pirate's Curse."

"The what?" Leo asked her with a shiver.

Liv rolled her eyes at her friends. "The Pirate's Curse, of course," she said. "When a pirate buries treasure, it gets cursed so that no one else can find it. Until the pirate wants it found."

"We know he'd like our community center idea," Elizabeth said.

Liv turned to her and exclaimed, "Blackbeard wanted you to find the treasure so you found the map. And he wanted us to help, so we found you."

Leo leaned in to Michael and said, "That's the silliest thing I've ever heard."

Michael shrugged. "I don't have a better answer, do you?"

They both laughed.

"Okay, then," Leo said. "I guess if Blackbeard the Pirate wants us to find his treasure, let's do it!"

Liv, Michael, Leo, and all the Teach family went house to house on Shaker Street.

"We can't just randomly dig more holes in people's yards," Liv said. "We need to knock on doors and ask permission."

"And we'll repair the damage we already did," Elizabeth Teach said. "We're sorry about that."

When the people on Shaker Street heard the story about the lost treasure and the family's plans, they all agreed to help. Even Sheriff Kawasaki came to help.

An hour later, using the map and the metal detector, Liv, Leo, and Michael had filled the Maker Sack with bags of Blackbeard's treasure.

They went with Elizabeth Teach and her family back to the Maker Shack.

"We're going to make you a security system for the house so you can protect your treasure," Michael told her. He started to dig through boxes. "We'll need feathers, glue, candles, mousetraps . . ."

• • •

When Elizabeth Teach went home, Michael said to his friends, "Good work! We solved a mystery."

"And helped Blackbeard's family," Liv said. "Plus, we protected alien energy cells."

"There are no aliens," Michael told her. "I thought we agreed about that."

"I never agreed," Liv told him. She still had Elizabeth Teach's map. "I counted all the holes she dug. And guess what?"

"What?" Michael and Leo asked together.

"There are way more holes out there than Elizabeth Teach and her family dug," Liv said. "I figure that the Martians must have a new fuel that isn't metal. That's why we can't detect it."

She poked her finger on the map. "They hid their cells in the extra holes," she concluded.

"Impossible," Michael told her.

"I'll prove it," Liv told him. "Tonight. After it's dark. We'll use my new telescope to watch the sky. We can send signals to outer space with Leo's headlamp." She grinned. "We'll find a way to tell the Martians we want to live in peace. We'll be intergalactic heroes."

"Aliens, ugh." Leo was a little scared.

Michael laughed. "Okay," he told Liv. "If you can prove to me that Martians are real, I'll wear red clothes for a whole week!"

"Deal," Liv said.

# YOU CAN BE A MYSTERIOUS MAKER TOO:

## MYSTERY-SOLVING METAL DETECTOR

### Things to find:

- Calculator
- AM radio
- Strong tape (like duct tape)

### What you do:

1. Turn the radio on. Set it to the high end of the AM band, where you hear static. Avoid all radio stations.
2. Turn the volume up all the way.
3. Hold the calculator next to the radio until you hear a loud sound. Move the calculator up and down on the radio.
4. When you hear an even sound, tape the calculator and radio together. Now you have a metal detector!
5. Check it out by placing the metal detector near a metal spoon or something else that is metal. The radio will beep if it is working correctly.
6. Go search for treasure!

# INVISIBLE INK

## Things to find:

- Lemon
- Bowl
- Water
- Q-tip or paintbrush
- White paper

## What you do:

1. Squeeze the lemon juice into a bowl.
2. Add a few drops of water and stir.
3. Using the Q-tip or paintbrush, write your message on the paper. Wait for it to dry.

## To read the message:

1. Hold the paper over a hot light bulb or candle — be super careful! The message will reveal itself.
2. Send secret messages to your friends!

# ABOUT THE AUTHOR

Stacia Deutsch is the author of more than two hundred children's books, including the eight-book, award-winning, chapter book series Blast to the Past. Her résumé also includes Nancy Drew and the Clue Crew, The Boxcar Children, and Mean Ghouls. Stacia has also written junior movie tie-in novels for summer blockbuster films, including *Batman, The Dark Knight* and *The New York Times* best sellers *Cloudy with a Chance of Meatballs Jr.* and *The Smurfs*. She earned her MFA from Western State where she currently teaches fiction writing.

# ABOUT THE ILLUSTRATOR

Robin Boyden works as an illustrator, writer, and designer and is based in Bristol, England. He has first-class BA honors in Illustration from the University of Falmouth and an MA in Art and Design from the University of Hertfordshire. He has worked with a number of clients in the editorial and publishing sectors, including Bloomsbury Publishing, *The Phoenix* comic, BBC, *The Guardian*, *The Times*, Oxford University Press, and Usborne Publishing.

# GLOSSARY

**capsule** (KAP-suhl)—a small case, envelope, or covering to hold something

**colonize** (KAH-luh-nize)—establish a group of people to live in a new place

**compound** (KAHM-pound)—substance made from two or more chemical elements

**concave** (kahn-KAVE)—curved inward, like the inside of a bowl

**convex** (kahn-VEKS)—curved outward, like the outside of a bowl

**descendant** (di-SEN-duhnt)—someone who is related to a specific ancestor

**intergalactic** (in-ter-guh-LAK-tik)—existing or occurring in the space between galaxies

**podcast** (PAHD-kast)—a program supplied on the Internet for watching or listening to on a mobile device or on a computer

**radiation** (ray-dee-AY-shun)—particles that are sent out from a radioactive substance; radiation can be harmful to lifeforms

**radio wave** (RAY-dee-oh WAVE)—an electromagnetic wave with radio frequency

# TALK WITH YOUR FELLOW MAKERS!

1. Which facts do Michael and Leo find to prove to Liv that aliens don't exist? Do you think Liv accepts those facts? Does she change her mind?

2. What are Liv's reasons for believing in aliens? Which sources does she get her information from? Do you think these are accurate sources?

3. The Mysterious Makers of Shaker Street consider themselves a great team. What are some characteristics of a good team? Which characteristics do Michael, Leo, and Liv each bring to the team?

# GRAB YOUR MAKER NOTEBOOK!

1. The Mysterious Makers discover that aliens have not visited Shaker Street. Using the original clues they find, rewrite the ending of the book as if aliens really had visited.

2. How do we know that Elizabeth Teach is related to Blackbeard the Pirate? Write about what it would be like if you were Blackbeard's descendant. How would your life be different from the way it is now?

# THE FUN DOESN'T STOP HERE:

Discover more at www.capstonekids.com

- Videos & Contests
- Games & Puzzles
- Friends & Favorites
- Authors & Illustrators

Find cool websites and more books like this one at www.facthound.com. Just type in the Book ID: 9781496546791 and you're ready to go!

# READ MORE MAKERS ADVENTURES!